Mrs. Lather's Laundry

By Allan Ahlberg
Illustrated by André Amstutz

GOLDEN PRESS • NEW YORK
Western Publishing Company, Inc.
Racine, Wisconsin

First published in the United Kingdom by Puffin Books/Kestrel Books.
Published in the U.S.A. in 1982.

Library of Congress Catalog Card Number: 81-84152
ISBN 0-307-31705-6 / ISBN 0-307-61705-X (lib. bdg.)
A B C D E F G H I J

Monday was a bad day
in Mrs. Lather's Laundry.
Mr. Lather was having trouble
with the ironing.

Miss Lather and Master Lather
were having a tug-of-war
with the washing.

Mrs. Lather was going crazy.
"If I wash one more sock,
 I will go out of my mind!" she said.
"I am sick of socks.
 I hate them!"

After that Mr. Lather put a notice
in the laundry window.
It said:

Tuesday was another bad day
in Mrs. Lather's Laundry.
Mr. Lather was having trouble
with a sheet.

The children were playing
tennis in the washing.

Mrs. Lather was going crazy again.
"If I wash one more undershirt,
  I will go out of my mind!" she said.
"I am sick of undershirts.
  I hate them!"

   After that Mr. Lather put another
notice in the window.
It said:

WE WASH ANYTHING
EXCEPT SOCKS AND UNDERSHIRTS

Then Mrs. Lather said,
"And no trousers either!
Or blouses or dresses!
Or tablecloths! Or pajamas!
I am sick of all of them.
I hate them!"

After that the children put
a notice in the window.
It said:

WE WASH ANYTHING
EXCEPT LAUNDRY

Wednesday was a *quiet* day
in Mrs. Lather's Laundry.

But Thursday was a surprising day!
First a customer came in with a baby.
"We do not wash baby clothes,"
said Mrs. Lather.
"I do not want you to wash his clothes,"
said the customer.
"I want you to wash him!"
"Oh!" said Mrs. Lather.
And she washed the baby.

I want you to wash him!

After that more customers
came in with their babies.
There were old customers
and young customers.
There was a big customer
with a little baby.
There was a little customer
with a big baby.

And there were lots more customers besides.

At first Mrs. Lather washed the babies
and was very happy.

"I like washing babies," she said.
"I love them!"

But by the end of the day
she was sick of them.
And the notice in the window said:
WE WASH ANYTHING
EXCEPT LAUNDRY AND BABIES

Friday was another surprising day
in Mrs. Lather's Laundry.
A customer came in with a baby
and a dog.

   "We do not wash babies,"
said Mrs. Lather.

   "I do not want you to wash the baby,"
said the customer.
"I want you to wash the dog!"

   "Oh!" said Mrs. Lather.

I want you to wash the dog!

And lots more besides.

And she washed the dog.
    After that more customers
came with their dogs.
There were long dogs and short dogs;
happy dogs and sad dogs;
black, brown and spotted dogs.

At first Mrs. Lather
washed the dogs.
Then she got sick of them
and Mr. Lather washed them.
Then he got sick of them.

By the end of the day
the notice in the window said:
WE WASH ANYTHING
EXCEPT LAUNDRY,
BABIES AND DOGS

Saturday was the worst day of all
in Mrs. Lather's Laundry.
Mrs. Lather washed:

I want you to wash me.

a tramp,

a car,

a soccer team—

and an elephant!

Mr. Lather and the children
washed the elephant, too.
When they got sick of it—
the elephant washed them!

Sunday was a *good* day
in Mrs. Lather's Laundry.
The notice in the window said:
CLOSED

On Monday Mrs. Lather was feeling better.
  "Will you be going crazy today, Mom?"
the children asked.
  "No," said Mrs. Lather. "I feel better now."
She began to laugh. "After all—
what could be worse than an elephant?"

The End